KiDWiTNESS
T·A·L·E·S

THE
Worst Wish

LISSA HALLS JOHNSON

BETHANYHOUSE
MINNEAPOLIS, MINNESOTA

Worst Wish, by Lissa Halls Johnson
Copyright © 2000 by Focus on the Family
All rights reserved. International copyright secured.

Cover illustration by Chris Ellison
Cover design by Lookout Design Group, Inc.

This story is a work of fiction. With the exception of recognized historical figures, the characters are the product of the author's imagination. Any resemblance to any person, living or dead, is coincidental.

Unless otherwise identified, Scripture quotations are from the HOLY BIBLE, NEW INTERNATIONAL VERSION®. Copyright © 1973, 1978, 1984 by International Bible Society. Used by permission of Zondervan Publishing House. All rights reserved. The "NIV" and "New International Version" trademarks are registered in the United States Patent and Trademark Office by International Bible Society. Use of either trademark requires the permission of International Bible Society.

A Focus on the Family book
Published by Bethany House Publishers
A Ministry of Bethany Fellowship International
11400 Hampshire Avenue South
Bloomington, Minnesota 55438
www.bethanyhouse.com

Printed in the United States of America by
Bethany Press International, Bloomington, Minnesota 55438

Library of Congress Cataloging-in-Publication Data

Johnson, Lissa Halls, 1955–
    The worst wish / Lissa Halls Johnson
        p. cm. — (KidWitness tales)
    Summary: Angry with his pesky older sister, Seth wishes that she were dead and is horribly guilty when she gets sick and dies, but Rabbi Jesus is able to bring her back to life.
    ISBN 1–56179–882–7
    [1. Brothers and sisters—Fiction. 2. Raising of Jairus' daughter (Miracle)—Fiction. 3. Jesus Christ Miracles—Fiction. 4. Jews—Palestine—Fiction.]
I. Title. II. Series.
    PZ7.J63253 Wo 2000
    [Fic]—dc21   00-056447

3 4 5 6 7 8 9 10 11 12 13 14 15 / 07 06 05 04 03 02 01

For my siblings:
Tim, Mindy, and Shelly
I'm sure you wished to be rid of me
when I was a pesky kid
but I'm glad we're friends now.

LISSA HALLS JOHNSON is the author of thirteen novels for Young Adults, including the bestselling *Just Like Ice Cream* and the CHINA TATE SERIES for Focus on the Family.

As Seth leaned against the gnarled olive tree he could think of only two things he hated.

His pesky older sister, Tabitha.

And waiting.

Right now he was waiting—for his best friends. The only good thing was that Tabitha was nowhere in sight.

Yet.

Where are they? he wondered. He picked at the bark on the tree and waited some more. He wished it would cool down. As long as it was so hot, he knew he and David and Joshua would barely be able to plod through their homework assignment, leaving no time for anything fun.

A small cloud of dust caught his attention. He could see David approaching, trying to walk like his father always did—slow, dignified, his chin tilted up just a bit. David didn't look dignified, though. He just looked dumb.

"David," Seth called, "hurry up! Where's Joshua?"

David looked around, maybe to see if anyone would notice if he changed his stride. He broke into a trot, not looking any less dumb than before. "Joshua said to come meet him by the almond orchard," he called. "He's got something to show us."

"Do you know what it is?" Seth asked.

David slowed when he reached Seth, then shrugged. "If it's Joshua, it could be anything. But it's probably gross."

Seth laughed. Joshua, a fisherman's son, seemed to like gross things. He could gut a fish before Seth could even figure out where to puncture it with his knife. After gutting the fish, Joshua would be fascinated with how the fish was put together, while Seth just wanted to throw the stinky, slimy inside stuff away.

Heading toward the orchard with David, Seth glanced over at his friend. David walked like any other 10-year-old kid when he didn't think people were watching. Since he and Seth were almost the same size, they kept in step easily. They looked so much alike, with their brown, curly hair, that people often thought they were brothers. The only difference was that David's face was speckled with freckles, and Seth just had two—one on the end of his nose and one underneath his right eye.

It was good to have friends like David and Joshua, Seth thought. He couldn't imagine what he'd do without them. He hoped he'd never have to find out.

It took them a few minutes to find Joshua. Finally they saw him, looking tall and strong as ever, standing on the edge of a grove of trees. He was motioning them over, so excited he couldn't stand still. Either that, or he needed to go to the bathroom real bad, Seth thought.

"Don't come any closer," Joshua said, holding out his thick hands to warn them away. He looked behind himself as if whatever was there might disappear at any moment. His straight, dark hair stuck out every which way from his head. He'd probably been running his hands through it like he always did when he was impatient or getting really excited about something.

David stopped, glaring at Joshua. "So what is it?" he demanded.

Joshua smiled. "You have to guess." He dug his finger deep into his ear. When he brought it out, he studied it, then wiped it on his short summer tunic.

"I don't want to guess. I want to study," David said.

Joshua frowned. "That's all you ever do." He dug a finger into his other ear.

"I like learning," David said for the thousandth time.

I don't want to study and I don't want to guess, Seth thought. "You've found . . . a broken pot," he said, knowing and not caring that his answer was lame.

Joshua threw out his arms, the smile leaving his face. "You've got to be kidding! I wouldn't bring you all the way out here for a broken pot."

David's brows pulled together. He scrunched his eyes closed like he always did when he was thinking. Suddenly, his eyes flew open as he raised his hand in the air. "It's a scroll. You found an ancient scroll!"

Joshua shook his head, offended. "No."

"It's something horrible and disgusting," Seth suggested.

"You're close!" Joshua said, brightening.

"It's your scab collection," David muttered, his voice flat.

"No," Joshua said. "But I can show that to you later if you want."

"I'll skip it," David mumbled.

"Guess again!" Joshua shouted, flapping his arms around and turning in circles.

"If we don't hurry up and guess, I think he's going to fly apart," David warned.

"Yes! Yes!" Joshua screamed. "Hurry. I want to show you." He looked like he might explode at any moment.

"Well, show us then!" Seth ordered. "We can't guess, and I want to get through our homework assignment as soon as possible."

"Okay, okay," Joshua said, moving aside and pointing at an object on the ground. Seth and David came closer.

"Wow," David said, looking at the dead bird. "How do you think it died?"

Poor thing. Seth tilted his head, studying the broken carcass. *Dead things are so sad.*

"Isn't it great?" Joshua asked. He picked up a stick and began to poke and prod the dirty, feathered creature. As he moved it, white worms that looked like moving rice started to come out of it. "Ewww! Look at that. Must be hundreds of the little critters."

Seth grinned. Joshua's joy over gross things was funny. David didn't look joyful, though. He was studying the whole situation like he was trying to learn something.

Seth squatted down to get a better look. *Why do maggots eat dead things? Did God make maggots, too? Does God care about dead things? Or is He done with them once they're dead?* He picked up a stick and poked gently at the bird. The beak was open, and a thin, red tongue dangled toward the ground.

"Speaking of maggots," David said, "where's your sister today?"

Seth stared at the busy worms while Joshua moved the bird around. "I don't know. She won't bother us."

Joshua snickered. "She *always* bothers us."

Seth looked down. A smile crossed his face. "If she does, I know exactly what we can do." He looked up at his friends. "She hates maggots."

Joshua caught Seth's smile and nodded.

"I'm not touching those disgusting things,"

David said. "You guys are unclean as it is, touching that bird."

"Who's going to know?" Joshua asked. "You don't tell, and I won't."

"I *have* to tell," David said, acting like a smaller version of his father, a strict, religious man called a Pharisee. "If anyone breaks God's law, they must pay the price."

"Don't listen to David," Seth argued. "We're not unclean."

"You've touched a dead animal," David insisted. "God's law says that your family will have to sacrifice because you're unclean."

Joshua looked worried. "My dad will kill me."

Seth shook his head. "No, we only touched it with a stick. You aren't unclean if you just touch it with a stick. You have to touch it with your hands."

Joshua held up his hands, the stick dangling from his fingers. "I haven't touched it with my hands."

David shook his head. "Well, I still think you're unclean."

"Quit arguing," Seth said. "Let's get our assignment done so we can go down to the lake."

"We can do it here, can't we?" Joshua asked. "I

don't want to leave this bird."

"It *is* a little cooler here," Seth agreed.

David sat on a rock, then gathered some pebbles and small, jagged stones from around his seat. He turned to face a larger rock and pitched a small one at it. The smaller rock shattered. "Have Joshua recite first."

"You always make me go first!" Joshua complained.

"That's because you're always the worst," David said. "I wouldn't want you to feel bad if I went first and did better than you."

Joshua glared at David. Then he looked at Seth and shrugged. "I think my brain has stopped working," he announced.

"I don't think it ever started," David mumbled.

"Funny." Joshua kept looking at Seth. "Do you think your dad would let us skip a day of school-work?"

"No way. We'd be behind everyone else," Seth said. "He doesn't stop teaching even when he's at home."

"I'd hate being the synagogue ruler's son," Joshua said, using the stick to make the bird's wing go up and down. "All that teaching all the time. And you have to act nice and proper everywhere you go. Ugh!"

"I would love it," David replied. "You get to meet all the travelers who stay in the synagogue. You get to have dinner with most of the rabbis. Your father is the one who chooses which rabbi gets to read the Torah and explain it. What an honor!"

"Yeah, but then you have to listen to them all, too," Joshua added. "Boring ones like Rabbi Kohath."

The boys groaned in unison at the memory of the stuffy Rabbi's long-winded talks.

"He came to our house for dinner," Seth told them. "Even Mother almost fell asleep."

They all laughed.

"Well, there are good rabbis, too," Seth said. "Ones that are really interesting, but don't get a chance to read or speak. It's fun to listen to Father talk with them after dinner."

"I liked Rabbi Jesus," Joshua said, his eyes lighting up. "He likes fishermen."

David grunted. "My father says he talks like a know-it-all. He read the Torah—*God's* holy word to Moses—like it was his *own* words." He paused, then looked around as if making sure no one was listening. "But I liked his stories."

Seth sighed. He'd had a sore throat the day Rabbi Jesus read and spoke in synagogue. He was sorry he missed the stories.

"If my father were synagogue ruler, I would be very proud," David said. "But I don't think I'd want him as my teacher at school *and* home."

"I'm sure glad my dad's not *my* teacher," Joshua said. "Except about fishing, of course." He flipped the bird over and began poking it in the back.

Seth wiped the sweat from his face with a corner of the linen cloak that hung to his knees. "Listen. The sooner we get this memorized, the sooner we can go do something else." He looked longingly across the dried grass on the hill toward the lake below.

Joshua followed his gaze. "Why don't we just go to the lake and put our feet in?" he suggested. "We can throw rocks in the water and maybe we'll learn better."

Seth looked at him. "We tried that once, remember? We got in a water fight and that was the end of memorizing."

"My dad almost killed me for not knowing the verses better," David frowned.

"Okay, okay," Joshua said. "Then let's hurry up."

Seth looked at the lake again, wishing he could lie in the cool water, with only his face showing, staring up at the brilliant blue sky. He figured Joshua was thinking only about catching the next fish. David was probably the only one with his mind on the Torah.

"I think I've got it memorized," David said.

"Well, spit it out then," Joshua said. "Maybe it'll rub off on me."

Seth turned away from the lake, forcing himself to pay attention.

David stood, dusting off his backside. His brown eyes took on a vacant look, seeming to scan the trees for the words. He cleared his throat. "This is from the prophet Isaiah. 'Do not call to mind the former things, or ponder things of the past.' "

"Good goin'," Seth said, smiling. "Keep it up."

"I will if you be quiet," David said. "I can't think if you interrupt." He looked at the trees again and swallowed. "Behold I will do . . . uh . . . I will do a something . . . and you will not know it . . . no, that's not right . . ."

Suddenly a confident voice came from the grove

behind Joshua. ". . . Do not call to mind the former things, or ponder things of the past. Behold, I will do something new, now it will spring forth; will you not be aware of it? I will even make a roadway in the wilderness, rivers in the desert."

Seth dropped his head into his hands and groaned.

It can't be! he thought. *Not now!*

"Seth!" David shouted. "You promised she wouldn't come! Why is she here?"

"I don't know," Seth mumbled, feeling as hopeless as a certain pile of feathers on the ground.

Seth looked up at the same moment his older sister saw the bird.

"Ugh! Maggots!" Tabitha shrieked. She backed up so fast she ran into a tree.

"Want some?" Joshua said, catching a few on the end of the stick and flinging them toward her.

Tabitha shrieked again and jumped out of the way.

"Why don't you go fall in the well, Tabitha?" Seth said.

"NO!" she said, crossing her arms.

Joshua flicked more maggots toward her.

She flinched. "I'm not moving," she said.

"Make her leave," David said.

"I don't have to leave if I don't want to!" Tabitha replied. "I can go anywhere I want." She stood with her arms crossed. Her long, brown hair hung loosely about her shoulders. Her dark brown eyes glared at them, daring them to force her to do anything.

Everyone looked at Seth. He stared at the ground but could feel their eyes on him. He could also feel his cheeks flushing. The thought of his friends seeing him embarrassed made him even *more* embarrassed.

You're the man *here, Seth*, he told himself. *You are the firstborn male. She may be a lot taller, but you have a right to tell her what to do.* Seth lifted his chin and pretended to have the authority he didn't feel. "We are reciting Torah, so you must leave," he said.

"And not doing a very good job of it," Tabitha added.

David and Joshua muttered something Seth couldn't hear. He clenched his teeth and his fist. He wanted to hurt her, but he couldn't.

He took a few deep breaths, then spoke. "We're still learning. And because we are trying to do lessons our *father* assigned us in school, I really think you should go."

"Come on, Seth," Tabitha said, exasperated. "Just let me stay and listen. I'll keep quiet, honest."

"No." Seth kicked at the dirt, sending up a cloud of dust. "Just go away!"

Tabitha turned up her nose. "I like it here." Dropping to the ground, she crossed her arms.

"We don't like you here," Seth said. "*Father* wouldn't like you here."

"The *maggots* don't like you here," Joshua said.

David nodded in agreement.

Seth took a step in her direction, and his nose twitched. It tickled. He took in a deep breath and choked. "Besides, you stink."

"I don't stink," Tabitha protested. "I smell pretty."

"I'm with you, Seth," Joshua said. "I think she stinks."

Tabitha stuck her tongue out at Joshua. "What do you know? You're only 10. And you stink like fish."

"I know more of the Torah than you," Joshua replied.

"Prove it," Tabitha said.

"Why are you wearing perfume?" Seth interrupted. "Does Mom know?"

"I'm almost 13," Tabitha said, tipping her head back. "It's time I started to look and act my age."

David rolled his eyes. "As if anyone but you cares."

"Eli cares," Tabitha said, her cheeks turning red.

"That old goat? He must be at least 24 years old," David said. "He's so blind, he'd fall in love with a donkey if it smelled right."

Seth and Joshua howled.

"At least Eli can recite Torah properly," Tabitha countered, her eyes flashing fire. "I'd rather marry an old goat like him than a little boy like you."

"He's studied Torah for years," David argued. "If he *didn't* know it better, he'd be the laughingstock of Capernaum."

"And all Galilee *and* Judea," Joshua added.

"Which is what our family will be if you keep trying to be a boy," Seth said bravely. He hated the thought of everyone laughing at his family behind their backs. His father would be especially embarrassed. It would be horrible to have his daughter bring him shame.

"I am not trying to be a boy," Tabitha said, her eyes welling with angry tears. "I just want to go to school. I want to learn."

"And you think old Eli would like it if you did?" Seth asked.

"I don't care what he thinks."

"I thought you did," David said.

For a moment she looked flustered, then frowned. "I mean I don't care what people think when it comes to me learning things. At least Mom understands. She teaches me what Father has taught her."

At the same instant, all three boys' mouths dropped open.

"Can women learn?" Joshua asked, letting go of his stick and apparently forgetting the bird.

"Do they even *want* to?" David asked, his words barely audible. "My mom only knows the basic stuff. She leaves the room when my father and I discuss my lessons."

Seth couldn't speak. He'd heard whisperings coming from his parents' room long into the night. But he'd had no idea his father was teaching his mother.

It wasn't that women weren't supposed to learn things, he thought. It was just sort of presumed that most women didn't care. And once they became wives and mothers, then teaching them about Torah seemed pointless—except for the things most important for daily living and passing on to the children.

His obvious shock seemed to make Tabitha taller. "It's not against the law, you know," she said. "Mom told me I could come listen to you."

"I don't believe you," Seth said, hoping his words covered how unsure he felt. "I don't think you belong here, and neither do David and Joshua."

Tabitha let a slow smile cross her face as she stood up. "I'll be around," she said. "Do you really think you *little* boys can scare me away?" She winked at them. "Remember. I know you are unclean. Don't you think your parents would want to know?"

"I am *not* unclean!" David announced, indignant.

"We aren't, either!" Joshua said.

"We didn't touch the bird," Seth added. "Not with our hands." *Why is it that when I say it to Tabitha, I feel unclean?*

"I don't think that matters," Tabitha said. "Dead is dead. Unclean is unclean."

Seth glared at her and shook his head. He knew what she was doing. David wouldn't tattle on his friends, but Tabitha would force the issue.

"So can I stay?" She stood with her arms crossed, her right foot planted off to one side.

"Okay," Seth grumbled, hoping that would keep her from talking to any parents.

"No!" David said firmly. "I will *not* recite Torah around a girl."

"You can't make me do what I don't want to do," Tabitha announced.

The boys glared at her. She was right, of course. Joshua dug the stick into the squirming maggots. Seth could tell he was considering tossing more at her. Making her unclean. But then, he would be guilty, too.

"That's okay," she said with a smirk. "I have to go anyway. I'm sure Eli would like some help in the field."

Seth hated that smirk. He hated the way she stood. She knew exactly what she was doing—ruining his life. And worse, she *enjoyed* it.

She turned on her toe, so slowly that Seth wondered if she would really leave. She moved away gradually, glancing back over her shoulder and looking at each boy. "See you soon."

When she was finally out of earshot, David looked squarely at Seth. "Are you sure you want friends?"

Seth looked at David, his stomach getting

fluttery inside. "What do you mean?"

"You heard me," David said, lifting his chin slightly.

Seth could feel his heart starting to beat faster. "We've been friends almost since the day we were born. Why wouldn't I want to be your friends?"

"I just wondered," David said, "because you don't seem to need any."

"I don't understand." Seth swallowed hard. The truth was he *hoped* he didn't understand.

"It's your sister, locust-face," Joshua added. He picked up a beetle, letting it crawl over his finger. "Seems to us like you would rather be with her." He set the beetle on a rock and quickly smashed it with another.

The blood drained from Seth's face. "No, of course not."

"I don't want anyone as my friend who likes to stick around girls," David said. He stood in front of Seth, his chest puffed out.

"Come on. You have pesky brothers and sisters too," Seth argued. "What's the difference?"

"Wherever you go, there *she* is." Joshua jerked his head in the direction of the small dust clouds Tabitha's sandals kicked up. He stepped next to

David, adopting the same stance. "At least *our* brothers and sisters stay out of the way."

Seth's stomach bounced and flipped and turned over and over. "You'll give me another chance, won't you?" he said, his voice barely coming out in a whisper.

David and Joshua looked at each other, seeming to trade thoughts without trading words. David turned to Seth. "We've been talking."

Seth didn't know if he wanted to hear what was coming next. His heart picked up its pace.

Joshua dug his finger into his ear. He looked at it, then wiped his finger on his clothes. "If this keeps up, we don't know if we want to be around you anymore."

Seth gulped. *No friends?* The days would be torture—not just long and hot, but boring, too. *They won't. They can't.* But when he saw their angry faces, his heart skipped a beat.

Joshua squinted up at the sky. "It's not like we haven't given you a lot of chances."

"She listens in on everything we say," David said.

"She follows us around and says stupid things," Joshua added.

"She gets in the middle and just stands there so

we can't shoot our slingshots."

"When we play hide and find, she tells where everyone is."

"When we're counting, she off-counts so we'll get confused and have to start over," David declared. "And that's not all. We'd be here until Rosh Hashanah if we said everything she's done."

Seth nodded grimly. Everything they said was true. In the old days his sister had only bothered them every few weeks or so. But lately she'd been coming around almost every day. Sometimes she acted like she was their mother. Sometimes she acted like a little girl. She was a grown-up one minute and a little kid the next.

Why couldn't she be like his friends' sisters? They might run up to ask something, deliver a message, or bring a jar of water. But they never hung around. One look from their brothers and they would be off, sometimes giggling behind their hands. *Their* sisters didn't try to teach them Torah or show them up. *Their* sisters acted like girls were supposed to. *His* sister was an embarrassment, a bother, a pain the size of Mount Hermon.

Seth scooped up a sharp rock from the ground. He rolled the rock around in his hand, feeling the jagged edges. He willed himself not to throw it at his sister, who had stopped just out of hearing. He clenched his jaw so tight his teeth hurt. He spun on his heels and heaved the rock so hard, it shattered on the target rock.

"Good one," David said.

"I wish it had shattered on her head," Seth said.

The other boys nodded their agreement.

CHAPTER 3

Seth dragged himself home. He hated every rock, every stone, every tree he saw. He hated them all, and he didn't know why.

Prove it, David and Joshua had said. *Prove you don't like your sister more than you like us. Prove you're a guy like one of us.*

What did he need to prove? Did he like his sister more than his friends? *No! I have much more fun with my friends than with Tabitha! She's boring. She likes stupid things. She's a girl. She'll never know Torah.*

He picked up a rock, threw it at a tree, and missed. *Well, she* may *know Torah, but she shouldn't.* Girls were only supposed to know enough Torah to help them behave and to teach their children well. Maybe there was no law that said that, but . . .

He kicked another rock. It bounced down the path. *I wish Tabitha could get in trouble for knowing too much. That would be nice.*

But he knew it wouldn't happen. He kicked the rock again. Instead of flying out in front of him, it stuck itself deeper into the dirt. *Just like me. Stuck. How am I going to prove to my friends how important they are to me?*

They had given him one week to come up with something—and do it.

Seth shuffled into the courtyard of his family's home. His mother, slender and brown-haired, sat cross-legged on a mat, pouring grain into the center of two round, flat stones. She grabbed hold of a stick that was stuck into the hole of the top stone and began turning the mill.

The shade of the old olive tree draped a cool blanket of air over her. Even so, sweat stood out on her upper lip and forehead. She wore her simple work dress; the only time she wore her purple tunic with the embroidered sash was on the Sabbath, when they went to synagogue. Seth thought she looked pretty when she wore her purple tunic, and wished she could wear it every day.

Without even a greeting, Seth blurted, "Tabitha's

already talked to you, hasn't she? What did she say this time?"

He hoped Tabitha hadn't told his mother about the bird. His sister was always telling their mother stories about him and his friends. *I wish she'd tell the good things, too. Like when we helped the old crippled woman when she fell. Or when we gathered the quail that escaped from Sarai's basket.* No, Tabitha only told the bad stories, the stupid things.

"What she said is not important," his mother said, brushing a stray strand of hair out of her eyes.

"It is to me. She's always lying about me."

"Is everything she has ever told me about you a lie?"

Seth stared at the ground. "No."

"Then she doesn't *always* lie, does she?" His mother's voice was soft. She hardly ever raised her voice to anyone for any reason. It was just one of the things he liked about his mother. She might not be the loudest in the village, but she was the best.

"No," he said, his voice soft, matching hers. "Tabitha doesn't always lie."

His mother nodded. She added more grain and turned the flat wheels. The wheels crushed the grain between them.

He watched, remembering his sister's taunts, her refusal to leave them alone, and his anger flashed. "I hate her," he announced.

"Seth," his mother said, looking up briefly. "You don't hate her."

He remembered that David and Joshua didn't want to be his friends anymore. "I do hate her."

"What does she do that is bad enough to hate?" she asked.

"She spies on us, then makes fun of us later." Seth plopped down in front of her. He dug his toes into the soft dirt.

"If you don't talk about foolish things, she will have nothing to tease you about."

"She finds a way to tease us about Torah."

His mother's worn, sun-darkened hands continued to turn the stones. Flour began to spill out from between them. She looked at the emerging powder as she spoke. "I have talked to her about that. She won't do it again."

"But, Mother! What about her coming and trying to do things only boys should do?"

A wistful smile crossed her face. It was the same one that appeared whenever she was about to tell him something from her own childhood. This time, though, she did not tell a story. She stopped her grinding and looked at him, still smiling. "If you let her join you, she might become bored and leave."

"No, she wouldn't." Seth didn't like the churning in his stomach. He didn't like the bad taste in his mouth. He didn't like his sister.

"She is your only sister."

"A good thing," Seth mumbled.

"What was that, Seth? I didn't hear you."

"Nothing, Mother."

"Where is your gratitude to God that you have a sister?" She poured more grain into the stones.

"Does God want us to be grateful for things that are bad?"

His mother stopped her grinding and looked into his eyes. "You know the answer to that, Seth."

Seth sighed. *I know the answer, all right. I hate the answer as much as I hate Tabitha.* He wanted to spit in the dirt, but couldn't. He knew he was supposed to be grateful for all God gave. The God who gives good things. The God who allows bad. They were to always be grateful.

But Seth couldn't stop there. "Should we be grateful even for sisters who make us lose our friends?"

The grinding stopped. She looked at Seth with such love, he had to look away. "It would hurt to lose friends, but it would hurt worse to lose a sister."

Seth stared at the ground. He thought about that, but it didn't seem right. It would hurt more to lose his friends, he knew it.

His mother cupped her hand underneath his chin and raised his face to look at her. "If your friends would ask you to choose between them and your sister, they aren't good friends at all. And if you would lose them simply because your sister can be a pest sometimes, they can't be very good friends."

She let go of his chin and went back to her work. "Here, gather the flour and I'll make your favorite bread."

Seth's eyebrows rose. *She called Tabitha a pest?* He took a clay bowl and began to scoop up the flour from the tray around the millstones.

"Your sister won't always be in this house. She'll be betrothed soon, and then she'll be married. You'll miss her when she's gone."

Seth couldn't imagine that. She couldn't leave soon enough. And miss her? He planned to throw a party when she left! But he said nothing.

He watched the expressions on his mother's face

change as she continued grinding. There was a frown, then a slight smile. She didn't look up as she spoke. "If you don't like how things are going with your sister, you can change it."

"How?" Seth stopped scooping flour. "I've tried to change her. I've asked her to stop. I've asked her to go away. Nothing works."

"I didn't say to change *her*. I said you need to change something in the way you get along."

Seth sat down and hugged his knees. "What am I supposed to do?"

His mother looked at him carefully, then back at her work. "What have you wanted to do?"

Seth didn't hesitate. "I would like to make a wall in our room so I don't have to see her."

His mother's knuckles turned white as she grasped the wood handle and turned it. "Do you think this is the way to change things?"

Yes! he wanted to shout. *Then I can pretend she doesn't exist!* Seth swallowed the words away, knowing his mother would not like that answer. "I think it might help," he said quietly.

His mother stopped grinding. She didn't look at Seth, but at the stones. Her small smile spread across her face. "Yes. You may make a wall in your room so you don't have to see her."

Seth stared at her. He hadn't expected his mother to agree. He'd thought for months about building a wall, but never thought he'd get to do it. He smiled to himself. His dream was about to come true!

Best of all, it'll prove to my friends that they're important, and Tabitha isn't!

"Tomorrow," his mother said, smiling as if she had some kind of secret. "You may start building to-morrow, after your studies."

CHAPTER 4

That night, as they usually did during the six hot and dry months, Seth and his family ate their evening meal in the courtyard. It was cooler and brighter outside. Seth liked it; he could stretch out a bit more. He didn't even mind helping his mother lay out the round reed mat upon which they put the dishes of food.

Tonight there was baked fish and fresh bread. To Seth, the smell was better than any perfume. It would only fill his nostrils, though. The food itself, cooked with dill and garlic and onion, would also fill his stomach.

After the hot food, there were split, juicy melons to share. The sticky juice would run down his face and arms, and he would be able to sprint down to the cool lake to wash it off. When he was younger, he liked playing in the dirt after eating a good melon. The dirt would stick to him in patterns and streaks. Then he and David and Joshua would chase after the smaller children until they screamed.

Seth looked at the spread and smiled. This was his favorite meal. *I wonder if Mother made this on purpose for me?*

When everything was ready, they all lay on their left sides. As required, Seth fingered the fringe at the bottom of his tunic to help him remember God's commandments while his father prayed: "Thanks be to Him, Lord our God, who has given us bread from the earth."

"Amen," the family said together.

Many times Seth did not feel close to this God. Yet when he prayed and let the knotted tassel that stood for the commandments of the Lord run through his fingers, he was again amazed that this powerful, almighty God had chosen the Israelites to be His people. Why would God choose *them* to give His law to? Why would He choose *them* to show His mighty power in battle after battle? It made him feel special and important. At these moments, nothing else mattered but God.

Tonight, the moment of closeness flew as soon as he opened his eyes. Since his parents weren't looking, Tabitha threw him a smirk. He knew exactly what it meant. She thought he was going to get into trouble for whatever she'd told their mother earlier.

But this time her sassy look didn't make him want to jump up and put his hands around her throat and shake some sense into her. This time when she smirked, he didn't feel like his fist might smack her a good one. This time he had a secret of his own. He hoped his return smile was more of a sneer. *I'm going to build a wall. So how do you like that one, my pesky sister?*

His sister tried her aggravating look several more times, but his return smiles confused her. Soon she looked uncomfortable.

Good, thought Seth.

Next came evening prayers and discussion, which Seth usually loved. It was a time when he had his father practically to himself. He could ask stupid questions and his friends wouldn't laugh—only Tabitha would. He could ask smart questions, and his friends wouldn't think he was showing off. He could listen to the wisdom of the Proverbs of King Solomon. He could give his ideas about the Messiah—who he might be, or when he might come.

At those times Seth would try to imitate the

gentle way his father moved his smooth, clean hands. Seth was proud of his father's hands. Because they were not singed brown by the sun, nor callused by hard labor, it meant his father was someone special, a respected elder in the community. Whenever he and his father walked through the village, and especially when they journeyed to towns farther away, Seth wanted to bring attention to his father's hands so everyone would know how special he was.

But tonight Seth could not concentrate.

"Esau gave up what?" Seth's father asked him.

"His birthright," Seth answered flatly.

"What was more important?" His father stroked his beard many times with his fine hands. Seth knew this meant he was getting frustrated.

"Food."

"Seth," his father said, "where are your questions? Where are your well-thought answers? The story of Jacob and Esau reminds us that God's laws are higher than our ways. We must learn how placing the wrong things above the right things—even for a few moments—can hurt us for the rest of our lives."

Seth nodded. But he wasn't really paying attention.

His father ran his fingers through his own curls, which were as thick as Seth's. Seth knew this meant he was about to be dismissed.

"Seth," his father said in his quiet tone. "If you cannot participate, perhaps it would be best for you to get along to bed."

It was intended as punishment, but Seth was glad for it. He could lie on his bed and dream of the wall he would build. "Yes, Father," he said.

He jumped up and moved from the courtyard toward the bedroom—a room just large enough for him and his sister to sleep in. *With a thin wall in between*, he thought. Passing Tabitha on the way, he couldn't miss the twist of her mouth and light of pleasure in her eyes—as if she'd won some unspoken game.

Glancing back, he watched as his sister sat on the mat he'd just vacated. "Father," she said, her voice filled with eagerness and wonder. "What do you think really happened at the Tower of Babel? Did families get to stay together?"

Tabitha was thrilled to have Father all to herself. Tonight Seth didn't care.

Entering the bedroom, he dropped to his lightly padded mat and lay on his back. He put his hands behind his neck and stared at the ceiling, not even trying to sleep. It was time to plan his wall.

He rolled over and lifted a few flagstones from the floor. He drew the outline of the wall in the dirt. He could see in his mind the digging he and his friends would do: They would laugh, and Joshua would get messy mixing the clay and water, and they would probably end up in a clay fight. David would drip with sweat, lifting heavy stones. They would work hard like real men.

It would be the best day.

Later, when Tabitha tiptoed into the room, he pretended to be asleep. He was still awake when she fell asleep. Listening to his sister's slow, easy breathing reminded him that soon he wouldn't hear that anymore. He wouldn't have to remember that his sister was in the room. He could stare at the wall and pretend.

Life was going to be sweet.

The next day in school, Seth kept yawning. His hands would smack together as if they had a life of their own. He'd get frustrated with them, and sit on them. But that didn't seem to help. Soon they'd be doing something else they shouldn't.

His father, a very patient man, glanced at him

occasionally, his eyes willing Seth to sit still and pay attention. But it seemed impossible. The fingers of one hand twined themselves with fingers on the other. They clasped and stretched so far forward that his elbows straightened out. His toe drew invisible designs on the cobblestone floor.

Seth looked around at the class, 23 boys of all ages, as his father asked a question. "What was Joseph accused of doing?"

Several hands shot up. Seth bit his lip and watched his toe. He knew the answer. He'd answered this one before. But his mind was filled with walls. Walls of Jericho. Walls for the Egyptians. Walls of water. *Now if Joseph had built a wall instead of . . . instead of . . . why can't I think of what it was he did?*

"What was the result of his actions?"

Seth stared at the raised hands around him. Who had answered the last question? What was the answer? He licked his dry lips. *We need a water break, Father*, he thought. That made him think about how much water they'd need to make the clay and dirt just right for building . . .

He looked over at David and Joshua, who also squirmed in their seats. He'd already told them about the wall. He looked at his father, who stroked his beard, and wondered whether the man would soon run his fingers through his hair and throw them out of synagogue school for the day.

That might not be such a bad thing, Seth thought. Then he sighed. If they left, the schoolwork would be difficult to make up.

Seth put on his best serious look. He drew his eyebrows together. He cupped his chin in his hand. He nodded when his father said something really important. But soon he discovered he was thinking about the height of the wall. Should they make it all in one day? Or would they have to let some of it dry before they began again? In the dark room, it would take longer to dry . . .

Hands went up and down around him. Voices spoke, brief moments of noise altering his thoughts.

"Joseph could have been stoned if the Law had already been in place," one student offered. *Stones. The best stones are along the shore just beyond where the boats rest.*

"Joseph never got a chance to prove he didn't do it," someone said behind him. *We all need a chance. A chance to dig. Joshua will want to dig the most. David will just get mad if he doesn't get a chance.*

His father's voice ran smoothly, like a stream without rocks. Seth let it wash over him without penetrating his thoughts. The only thing that pulled him back was hearing his name.

"Seth? How long was Joseph in prison?"

Seth's mouth went dry. He'd been caught.

Thinking fast, he decided that if he said some number confidently, it would at least look as though he'd been listening. "Six and one-half years."

Seth's father shook his head while the other boys snickered. "Please pay attention," his father said.

Seth sighed. He had to obey. He was the only boy in class who would have to deal with the results late into the night if he didn't.

His father moved toward him, then stood right in front of Seth. He peered at Seth again, his eyes boring right into his son's. The man stroked his beard, looking like a giant even though he wasn't very tall. Seth gulped, waiting for the fingers to go through the curls. Nervously he ran his fingers through his own hair.

Finally his father broke into a smile. He bent down and said softly, "Pay attention."

Seth nodded. He squirmed in his seat. *It won't be long now.*

CHAPTER 5

I'll get the water," was the first thing Joshua said when the boys gathered in Seth's room.

"That's a girl's job," David said.

"But I need it for a man's work," Joshua reminded him. "I'm going to build a wall."

They all grinned and slugged each other on the arm. They stared at the ground for a few moments, basking in the fun they were about to have.

"What are we going to do first?" David asked.

"Dig, you goat," Joshua said.

Seth spoke up. "First we have to gather what we need. David and I will find rocks, while you get the water."

The boys split up, and returned a short time later with their supplies.

Seth got to dig first, since it was his wall. As he plunged the shovel into the packed ground, a shiver of delight went through him. This, he thought, *will be all the proof they need.*

"Did you see all those people out there on the hill by the lake?" Joshua asked.

"How could anyone miss them?" David said.

"What do you think was going on?" Joshua said.

The boys looked at Seth for the answer. Since his father was the synagogue ruler, no community event happened without his father's knowledge—and usually not without his invitation and plan. Seth shrugged. "I don't know. Maybe it's just a traveling storyteller."

"Are you tired yet?" Joshua interrupted.

"No!" Seth said. "I'll let you have a turn in just a minute. Let me at least dig the outline."

"I hope it isn't that rabbi Jesus," David said. He started putting some of the discarded dirt into a bucket. "I mean, some think he's a good teacher and all, but . . ."

Joshua didn't hesitate to speak what he thought. "If he's telling his stories, all the people in town will block the streets. It'll be harder to get more water if we need it."

Seth frowned. He hadn't thought of that. Ever since Rabbi Jesus had chosen Capernaum for his temporary home, no one ever knew what would happen next. No one knew when he was going to be in town, and when he wasn't. He was kind of like the wind, some people said. You couldn't know when it might show up and make a mess of things. All three boys sighed and looked at each other.

Seth drew a line across the middle of the ditch he'd started. "Here. Your turn. Dig this half." Seth handed Joshua the shovel.

Joshua dug quickly, his portion done in no time. He handed David the shovel.

David kept talking. "I was going to say that too many people are believing what he says."

Seth added water to the bucket of dirt. "We really shouldn't say anything bad about a rabbi," he said.

"We weren't really," Joshua said quickly. "I just meant that today, it would kinda hamper our work if he was teaching. He really is a good teacher, though," he added. He paused. "Have you seen Peter the fisherman lately? My dad says he's gone most of the time following this rabbi. And when he does come back to fish, all he can talk about are all the things Jesus has done."

David leaned on the shovel and looked at Joshua

skeptically. "Does anyone believe Peter? He's always saying or doing something stupid. I sure wouldn't believe anything he says." He scooped out the last two shovels of dirt.

Joshua shrugged. "I don't know. The stories are pretty amazing. My dad seems to think Peter must be telling the truth." He scooped out some mud and plopped it in the hole.

"My father respects Rabbi Jesus," Seth told them as he laid the first stone in the ditch on top of the layer of mud. "He doesn't understand why so many of the others fight about Jesus all the time."

"I've heard he's healed people," Joshua said, packing mud around the stones Seth was placing in the shallow ditch.

"Really?" Seth asked. "I'd like to see that. But I've never even been in the right place to hear him tell a story."

David frowned. He put his hands behind his back and paced the small room. Five steps over. Five steps back. "My father says Jesus is nothing but trouble. He teaches things that aren't right."

"Aren't rabbis supposed to make us think?" Joshua asked, standing up to face David. "Aren't they supposed to get us to look at things differently?"

David lifted his chin. His eyes narrowed. "But when their words are blasphemy..."

Joshua tipped his head back and laughed. "He hasn't said anything that would make God less. He doesn't curse God or deny Him. He speaks of Him as though he knows Him very well. Just because he speaks the truth about Pharisees like your father..."

In a blur of flesh, fabric, and fist, Joshua was on the ground, rubbing his chin. David stood over him.

"Never talk about my father like that!"

Seth yanked David away. "Quit it! Let's finish building our wall. If talking about Jesus is going to cause fights, then let's find something else to talk about." He glared at each of his friends. "Got it?"

Both nodded.

"Let's work," Seth added.

Joshua bent over to slap some mud between the rocks. David and Seth exchanged a look. Seth picked up a wad of mud. He flung it at Joshua's backside. Thwack!

Without seeming to pay any attention to the wad of mud that hit him, Joshua flicked his wrist. Mud flew and smacked Seth's cheek. David dropped a rock on top of the other rocks, just a bit too hard, and mud pellets sprayed them all. "War!" Seth shouted, and soon they were all covered with mud.

After the war, it took them another two hours of singing loudly and badly, punching each other, and casually throwing a few more rounds of mud wads at each other before they had a nice wall about chest high. The mud in the wall began to dry quickly in the heat of the day, but they all knew it wasn't ready for the final coat. That would have to wait for tomorrow, after the inside of the wall had dried.

As they stood admiring their work and wondering what exactly to do next, they heard a gasp from the doorway. "What are you doing in my room?" Tabitha cried, her hands on her hips.

David and Joshua looked at Seth. Seth shook his head.

"Well?" she demanded.

"It's my room, too," Seth said.

She jerked her head at David and Joshua. "It's not theirs."

"I'm building a wall," Seth said, folding his arms across his chest.

"Why?"

David and Joshua started to snicker.

"So I don't have to look at you, or listen to you every night," Seth said. "It will be a constant reminder to you that I don't want you being a pest. That I don't want you around. That I don't even *like you*."

Seth looked at David and Joshua to see if his words were harsh enough for them. Surely this would be enough of a test of his friendship. *They'll see I'm their friend first, and a brother second.*

He was glad to see them smiling, with a sort of hardness around their eyes. It was as if they were ready for a battle—one they knew they would win.

Tabitha didn't move. Seth expected tears to form little pools in her eyes, like they always did when she wanted Seth to get in trouble. Then she would burst into full-blown crying and run to tattle on him. He waited.

Instead, her eyes narrowed. Her crossed arms tightened. She leaned forward. Seth and his friends leaned forward, too.

"You're all stupid!" she hissed, spittle spraying them all. "Do you think I care about what little smelly boys think?"

They jerked back, wiping their faces. As Seth's

arm moved away from his eyes, he saw her foot swing forward.

"No!" he shouted.

Seth reached his arm out to stop her, but it was too late. He and Joshua and David stood staring in horror as the wall tumbled into pieces at their feet. Clumps of mud flew about, sticking in globs on their arms, their legs, their clothes.

Tabitha stomped out into the sunshine.

The boys stared at the remains of their master-piece. Kneeling beside the ruins, Seth picked up a rock and examined it. The mud had been wet enough to crumble, but dry enough that the rocks wouldn't stick together again. The only way to re-build the wall would be to haul the rocks to the river, wash off the hardening mud, and start all over again.

"All our hard work," Seth said, his voice quaver-ing a lot more than he wanted it to. *Don't cry*, he told himself. *Then they'll* really *think you're a weak-ling.*

"Stupid!" David said, kicking at the one rock that remained on top of another. "If I was her father—"

Joshua interrupted. "What do you mean, if you

were her father? If I were her *brother* . . ." He let his voice trail off as he glared at Seth. His right fist slammed into his left palm, over and over.

"What?" Seth said, his mouth going dry.

"If I were her brother, I would have at least planted my fist in the middle of her face. I can't believe you let her get away with that."

Seth opened his mouth, but no words came out.

"You haven't done it yet, you know," David said.

"Done what?" Seth mumbled, his hope as crumpled as the wall.

"Proven to us that you can stand up to your sister," David replied.

Seth stood, pointing to the pile of rocks. "That was going to be it."

Joshua and David traded looks and began to laugh. "You're kidding, right?" Joshua asked. "That lousy wall wasn't what we had in mind."

"It has to be something public," David said.

"And humiliating," Joshua added.

David gave Seth a fake smile. "You have five more days."

The boys stepped over the mess and walked out of the house.

It took Seth half an hour to get the rubble out of

his room and haul it behind the house. When he was done, he went to the courtyard and sat in front of his mother.

He wanted to scream, but knew his mother wouldn't appreciate it. He put his head down so she wouldn't see the fire in his eyes.

She'd been working at the loom, watching him while he hauled the rocks. She'd said nothing. But he could tell she knew what had happened.

After a minute or so of silence had passed, Seth's mother spoke. "So what do you think this means?" she asked.

"If I knew, I wouldn't be here," he said, angry.

"What did you expect would happen?"

Seth picked up a stick and drew designs in the dirt. He shrugged his shoulders.

His mother said nothing. She sat still, her hands in her lap.

After a few moments, Seth said, "I thought she would leave me alone."

"What did I tell you that you needed to do?"

"Nothing."

"I told you that you needed to change something in the way you get along with her. I knew the wall wouldn't give you what you wanted."

"Then why did you let me build it?" Seth grumbled.

She smiled. "I knew you would learn something important."

"And what should I have learned?"

Again his mother sat silent, her hands still, her mouth restraining a smile.

Seth jabbed at the ground with his stick. He swirled it around quickly, destroying his dirt drawing. "Aren't you going to tell me?"

"No," she said.

He got up and began to walk toward the courtyard entrance.

"Come back and sit," she told him.

Seth stomped back and sat down hard, hoping his mother would see the unfairness of it all.

"Sit until you can understand what it is you have learned."

"I've learned not to listen to my mother," he blurted.

"Was it my idea to build the wall?"

"No."

"Think, Seth. Stay here until you know."

Seth swatted a gnat that kept trying to get close to his mouth. He knew his mother would make him stay until he figured it out.

Think. Think back. He forced himself to remember the conversation he'd had with her about building the wall. Well, it wasn't really about the wall. It was about doing something to make things better between Tabitha and him.

He sighed. "Building the wall didn't do anything to make things better. It only made things worse." He thought about what she would like to hear. "If I build a wall, it keeps Tabitha away from me. But it only makes her more mad. It doesn't make her nicer."

His mother clapped her hands once, her face breaking into a full grin. "Yes. Go and play. But think about what you can do to change what you say or do with your sister that doesn't keep her away, but honors her as your sister."

Seth walked into the street, letting his stick drag on the ground. He didn't want to think about what would honor his sister. He had to think of what he could do to humiliate her.

If he didn't, he would lose his friends.

Nothing could be worse than that.

CHAPTER 6

Prove it.

"How?" Seth said out loud as he hiked up the dirt path worn into the side of the hill. "How can I prove that I agree Tabitha is a pest? How can I prove my friends are most important?"

Usually he asked his friends for help on things like this. But this time he had to come up with something all by himself.

Tabitha hates to wear wet or dirty clothes. Seth bit his lip as he thought, then talked to himself. "If I got her soaking wet, then pushed her in the mud, she'd have to walk through town all filthy." He frowned. "No, she'd just rinse off in the lake. She'd be wet, but it wouldn't be enough."

He could dye her clothes blue or purple. But she might like that.

He could dye Eli's sheep—put different colored

spots all over them. No, that would make Eli mad, but it wouldn't really affect Tabitha.

His mind went blank. He couldn't think of anything else.

Looking over his shoulder, he saw the lake sparkling in the sun. He turned around and kept walking up the hill—backwards. He could see boats here and there. It looked so perfect from his place on the hill. Yet at any minute a storm could blow in and chew up the water something fierce.

Just like Tabitha, he thought. Things were perfect without her. Then she would come in and mess everything up.

How can I mess everything up for her? he wondered.

Turning, he continued up the hill to the very top. A breeze blew through the grass, making a shushing sound that almost sounded like the tiny waves that lapped the shore of the lake.

He found his favorite rock and sat on it, but soon he was fidgeting. He hated being alone. It was too quiet. Mostly, it was boring.

His mind seemed sluggish as he kept trying to think of things to do to Tabitha. Suddenly he realized he didn't *want* to do anything to her. He wanted her to leave him and his friends alone, but he didn't really want to do anything mean to her. He just longed to play with his friends—with nobody disturbing them.

I could tell David and Joshua to forget it, he thought. But then every day would be like today. Alone. Sitting on a rock. No one to test his skills against. No one to compete with. No one to recite with. No one to wrestle with.

I've got to think of something good.

He could remember something "good" that had happened to Tabitha once. They hadn't even planned it, but it was perfect.

He, David, and Joshua had been having a pomegranate seed-spitting contest, splattering a nearby rock with blood-red juice and white seeds. Tabitha had appeared after dark, bringing the message that the boys' mothers were looking for them. The boys convinced her to tell a scary story first, so she sat on a rock and told a tale that made them all shiver. Then, following her into town, they were astonished to see that red spots from hundreds of pomegranate seeds were speckling the back side of her robe, all the way down to the hem. She'd chosen the worst rock to sit on!

"She'll think we did it on purpose," David had whispered as they followed her. They'd all started snickering.

Tabitha had been embarrassed at first, and furious later. Seth had managed to convince his mother and father that he and his friends hadn't done anything wrong.

Now, sitting on the hilltop and staring at the water below, Seth wondered what his friends might want him to do. Would they be satisfied if Tabitha was just embarrassed? No. They wanted him to do something harsh. Something that would prove to her what a girl she was and how she didn't belong.

At that moment, he knew what he would do.

He climbed on top of the rock and jumped off. Then he ran down the mountain to find his friends.

———

Next day, the boys pooled their lunches. Joshua brought a fish broth. David brought a lamb stew. Seth told his mother he was extra hungry and brought a double portion of a lentil soup she'd made.

"Pour it in here," Seth said, holding out a clay pot. He picked up a stick from the ground and stirred the three together. "Anyone want to taste?" Seth asked.

David shook his head.

"Sure!" Joshua said. He took a drink. "Delicious."

"It's not supposed to be delicious," David complained. "It's supposed to be gross."

"But it should taste okay at first," Seth said. "We want her to eat it all until she gets to the special prize."

The boys all looked at each other and grinned.

Kneeling, Seth picked up a small handful of dirt. He dumped it into the pot and stirred, his heart starting to thump.

He removed a pouch from the cloth tied around his waist and crushed it against a rock. When he opened it, he saw the remains of several beetles and bugs mixed together. He put that into the pot, too, and stirred.

He looked up at David and Joshua. "Should we really do this?"

David nodded. "It's this—or you're on your own."

Seth swallowed. He forced a fake smile.

"It's your choice," David said. "Friends or not?"

Seth sighed and took another pouch from his waist. "I was going to save this for something else, but I guess it would go okay here." He opened the pouch and slipped in the special surprise.

Joshua's eyes grew especially bright. "This is going to be *real* good."

Moments later the boys were searching the town for Tabitha. They found her and some of her friends by the lake. *Perfect*, Seth thought. *This will please Joshua and David even more—an audience.*

"Hi," the boys said, greeting Tabitha and the other girls.

"We wanted to apologize," Seth said, trying to keep the apprehension out of his voice. "So we brought you a peace offering. We made it from the soups our mothers gave us for lunch." At that moment he felt sick inside and happy, all rolled into one.

Tabitha looked at them skeptically.

"It's good," Joshua said. "I tried it."

Tabitha took the pot. She smelled the soup. It had lost some of its warmth, but the aroma was still enticing. "Who made it?" she asked.

"My mother," David told her.

"Your mother is the best cook in town," Tabitha

said, still looking at the soup warily.

David beamed. "It's lamb."

Tabitha brightened. "I *love* lamb." Then she frowned. "It smells like fish, too."

"It's a new type of soup she's trying," David said. "Fish and lamb together. Soon all the women in Capernaum will be making it."

Seth bit his lip. He didn't want to say anything and mess everything up. He was afraid he'd shout, "Don't, Tabitha!" or that he would grab the pot and yank her head back by her hair and force it down her throat. He wanted her to dump it. He wanted her to drink it. Mostly, he wanted Joshua and David to always be his friends.

Tabitha looked at each of them. Then she took a tiny sip. She took another. Then she drank a lot more. "Thank you," she said. "I was famished, and this is good. And I don't have to go home to eat."

Tabitha passed her lunch around and the other girls each had a swallow.

Seth thought he was going to burst if she didn't get to the bottom soon.

"What are these dark things in it?" Tabitha asked.

"Special spices!" David said. Seth thought he sounded a bit too eager.

Tabitha continued to drink. When she neared the bottom, Joshua couldn't keep quiet any longer. "There's also dirt, a few mashed bugs, and . . ."

Joshua never got to the last ingredient. Tabitha screamed and dropped the pot. As it broke, a dead lizard rolled out, its soft, white belly shining in the sun.

Tabitha and her friends stared at the lizard. Tabitha clutched her stomach. Her eyes grew wide. She put her hand to her mouth, and her words could barely be heard. "There was a *lizard* in my soup."

Joshua and David laughed.

Seth winced. His sister's whimpering struck him deep inside. *You betrayed me*, she seemed to be saying.

Joshua nodded. "Isn't it cool?" He poked at the belly of the lizard. A little bit of soup squirted from its mouth.

Tabitha bent over, then emptied her stomach on the ground next to the creature. Her friends turned away, looking as if they were about to do the same.

David and Joshua set off at a run, and Seth followed. "You did it!" David declared over his shoulder.

Seth let relief take over, washing away all doubts over whether he had done the right thing. He joined in as the other boys laughed, and accepted their congratulatory slaps on his back.

That night at dinner Seth had his parents all to himself. At first he was nervous, certain Tabitha would tell on him.

"Tabitha's not feeling well," his mother had said.

"What's wrong with her?" Seth asked.

"Her stomach is unsettled. It's probably something she ate."

"What did she eat?" Seth asked, his heart pounding.

"Something some of her friends gave her."

His mother said nothing more about it. Seth wondered why Tabitha hadn't told. Then he smiled. *I guess we really did silence her. Success!* He couldn't stop smiling as he ate a double portion of fish and fruit that evening.

The next morning on the way to school, Seth could hardly contain his excitement. *It worked*, he thought, grinning. He felt so giddy. He kept punching David and Joshua until David said, "Quit it!"

Seth stuck his foot out and tripped Joshua, who fell
into the tall grass. Joshua reached up and pulled
Seth to the ground with him. They rolled around,
wrestling until Seth pinned Joshua.

I can't believe it, Seth thought. *Everything
worked perfectly.* Tabitha would know better than
to mess with *him* anymore. He put a swagger to his
walk, his chin in the air, and marched ahead of the
other two. "Hello, *boys*," he said to a group of
younger classmates.

The boys turned to look at him. Instead of looking at Seth as though he were a smarter, more important elder classmate, they looked at each other
and burst into laughter.

Seth turned to Joshua and David and shrugged.

Joshua popped a piece of dried fish into his
mouth. He spoke as he chewed. "I think I'm going
on the fishing boat again the day after Sabbath."

"How can you miss synagogue school?" David
asked, shocked.

"Father thinks learning my trade is more
important."

"There is nothing more important than God's
Word," David said in a lofty tone.

"Ah, but one must learn to be a man," Seth

added, feeling wise and important.

Joshua dug his finger into his ear as they waited for David's approval.

David shook his head. "The Law's the Law."

"Look," Joshua said, pointing at the younger boys, using the finger he had withdrawn from his ear. "Are they laughing at us?"

Seth shook his head. "Of course not. Why would they be laughing at us?" His happy feeling grew and grew. He wished he could make something that could float into the sky. He'd hold onto it and go up and up—just like his insides were doing right now.

"Then what's going on?" Joshua said, popping another piece of fish into his mouth.

"Probably laughing over something dumb," Seth said. "Little boys always laugh over dumb things."

As they got closer and closer to the synagogue, it seemed that *all* the boys around them were laughing about something.

"What are we missing?" Joshua finally said to one group of young boys. They didn't answer, but laughed even harder and ran.

"Baby," said a voice behind them. They turned to see a group of older boys snickering.

"I didn't know you wet your bed, David. A big holy boy like you?"

David's face grew dark.

"Is that why your father is always offering sacrifices? Because of his unclean son?"

"That's not true," Joshua defended his friend.

"Yeah, nose-picker?" taunted another boy. "We heard you have such a problem that your mother puts cloths over your hands at night."

Joshua's mouth flapped open and closed like a fish's.

"What is wrong with you guys?" Seth said. "Why are you making up these things?"

"No one's making up anything," the largest boy said. "Thanks to your sister Tabitha, we know all the interesting things about you."

"Like you suck your thumb sometimes when you sleep," the boy next to him said.

Seth's head swam. Everything felt jumbled in his head. He wanted to deny it—but he couldn't. He *had* sucked his thumb in the middle of the night when he'd awakened, scared.

He tried changing the subject. "What makes you think you know anything? You don't know if anything Tabitha said is true."

The big boy laughed. "You forget she is a woman. And all women talk. They talk while they wash clothes. They talk while they cook together, while they weave together. And I guess Tabitha just listens well."

"She's making sure all the kids in the synagogue know all your secrets," a small but older boy said.

With a final round of laughter, the boys moved past Seth and David and Joshua.

David and Joshua moved in front of Seth and stopped. Joshua's arms looked larger, his legs longer and stronger as he stood like a soldier defending something. David crossed his arms and his eyebrows drew together.

"No more!" Joshua said. "I'm not going to hang around with some kid whose sister tells things about *me*. Don't even *think* about being my friend anymore."

David glared. "Enough! I've had enough!" Without another word, they turned toward the synagogue and walked quickly away.

Seth stared after them. The further they got from him, the emptier he felt. He wanted to run after them, but he knew it was over.

Other boys on their way to the synagogue passed

him, laughing as they went. Did they believe what Tabitha had said about him?

He barely made it through synagogue school. He was glad they had a visiting rabbi who taught them his own interpretation of Scripture. Visiting rabbis usually didn't pay as much attention to the boys. Seth had the chance to sit and think.

What am I going to do without my friends? Seth pictured long afternoons trying to remember and recite Scripture alone. He pictured hot days without anyone to pitch rocks with him. He thought about rainy days alone in his house. Alone with *women.*

Tabitha did it. Tabitha has ruined me. Anger began to seep in. It began to grow stronger and warmer with each thought.

Seth couldn't wait until school was over.

Tabitha sat outside the courtyard of their home. She was embroidering some piece of linen, but Seth didn't care what she was doing. He stomped over to her and stood with his arms crossed. "You have ruined my life!" he told her.

Tabitha looked up at him, smiling sweetly. "You know I like games, Seth. And it seems you wanted to play the revenge game."

He was so angry, he could feel his crossed arms start to shake. Everything seemed to go white. Through a pinhole of sight he could see Tabitha's grin as she began to laugh.

Knowing—but not caring—that he was about to get into big trouble, Seth drew back his arm. With all the force he could muster, he slammed his fist into his sister's arm and followed with a kick to her shin.

Tabitha's laugh turned into a howl of pain.

Instead of running away to postpone getting in trouble as he usually did, Seth stood still. He wanted to see her hurting. *She deserves it*, he thought.

"*Mother!*" Tabitha screamed.

A moment later Seth's mother appeared, her hand holding up her robe so she didn't trip as she ran. Her face showed a mother's fear. "What happened, Tabitha? Are you all right?" She examined her daughter, apparently checking for blood.

Seth straightened himself as tall as he could manage. "I hit her."

Mother slowly turned and looked at him, her fear turning to anger. "You what?"

"She deserved it. She's ruined my life!" The rage

continued to pulse through him. His breath came in rapid, short bursts as if he'd been running a long distance.

"Has God given up His throne to you?" his mother asked.

Seth's brows pulled together, confused as he was by the question. "Of course not."

"Yet you take revenge into your own hands? It is only for God to decide whether or not there should be revenge. He also is the only One who decides what kind of revenge there should be. Anyone who takes revenge into his own hands has decided to become a god."

Not this time, Seth thought. God hadn't acted soon enough. God had not done His job.

"Go to your father and tell him what you have done," his mother said.

Tabitha's tears had stopped. She rubbed her arm.

Seth could tell she held back a smile. He glared at her, turned, and started toward the synagogue.

CHAPTER 7

Seth walked quickly past Capernaum's houses and groups of houses called *insulae*, powered by an energy that churned in him. It was as though one of the violent storms that gathered over Galilee had swirled around and gotten sucked inside him. Lightning bolts of thought lit up his mind. He could see Tabitha's smirking face with each bolt.

Thunderous anger rumbled through him. He wished it could come out in a way that would make her hurt as much as he did.

So Mother wanted him to be more understanding toward his sister, did she? He'd been understanding long enough. He'd endured her bossy ways for as long as he could remember. He'd listened to her tattle on him about stupid things, as well as things he really shouldn't have done.

A soft rain started to fall. He marched on,

getting as mad at the rain as he was at his sister. Why did it have to rain now? The drops felt hot and sticky, not cool and cleansing like a winter rain. Each drop watered his anger, making it grow like a weed.

Pictures flashed through his mind, pictures of everything his sister had done to irritate him, pick at him—torture him. *That's what it is*, he thought. *Torture*.

If she'd ever been even a little bit sorry, he probably could have let some of his anger go. But she never was. The thing was, she *enjoyed* pestering him.

Pictures of Tabitha's smirking face taunted him over and over. He clenched his fists. His breath came in shorter and shorter bursts. *How dare she! How dare she ruin my life!*

He kicked over a water pot, wishing it would shatter on the ground. He walked by a tail of onions hanging out to dry. He punched it so hard the strand flew apart and the onions scattered, rolling across the rain-spotted dirt.

He started to trot, then broke into a run. He could see the synagogue on the hill, growing closer with each step. He didn't want to get there. He didn't want to see his father and be put to work. He didn't want to have to come before his father and see the disappointment on his face.

He also didn't want to spew anger on his father. That would not be accepted, not for one minute. His father controlled anger, letting his jaw muscles work on the problem until he could speak of it without letting the wrong words fly from his mouth. Any outburst from Seth would be reprimanded.

He made a sharp turn and ran up the hill, leaving the town behind. *I hate her*, he thought. *I hate her more than . . .*

The truth was that, at the moment, he couldn't think of anything else he hated more.

He ran to the top of the hill, anger driving him, forcing him. He didn't care that his lungs hurt. He didn't care that his muscles screamed at him to take it easy. None of the pain compared to the hurt of losing his friends, of being made to look like a fool in front of all the other boys. *I hate her,* he repeated.

When he reached the top he stood in the rain, arms swinging, as if he could punch the raindrops. He slapped at them. He kicked the rocks. He didn't care that his sandals might be ruined. "I hate her!" he said aloud, the rain dripping down his face. Then he shouted at the top of his lungs, "I hate her, God! I hate her! I . . . *I wish she was dead!*"

For a moment it felt like the truest thing he had ever said in his life. He tipped his face toward the gray sky and said it again: "I wish Tabitha was as dead as that bird! No, I wish she was *more* dead!"

As he said the words, an eerie sort of peace came over him. The anger was still there, but something about voicing the words felt very good.

He moved down the hill slowly, cherishing the words. *I hate her.* He planted his feet carefully, one word for every step. *I wish she was dead.* He smiled to himself.

By the time he reached the synagogue, the rain had made mud in the streets. He took off his sandals underneath the portico of the synagogue. The roof stuck out over stones carefully set into the ground. Unless the wind blew the rain, it stayed dry there.

Seth found his father in the largest room of the synagogue, the room where they held the Sabbath services. "Hello, Father," he said.

"Seth!" his father exclaimed. "You have finally come to help the old man, huh? Come to keep me company in my work?"

Seth wished he felt sorry, but he didn't. He hung

his head anyway. It wouldn't hurt to at least *fake* being sorry. "Mother sent me," he said, as if talking to the ground. "I'm in trouble."

Seth looked up in time to see his father's look of joy turn to one of disappointment. Usually seeing that look on his father's face would be enough to dispel his anger and bring about a true sense of sorrow, but not this time. Tabitha deserved more than what he had given her. She probably didn't deserve to die, but he wished she would.

Without a sound his father gave Seth the broom and left the large room. *I hate sweeping, and Father knows it. This is Tabitha's fault, too.*

Seth began to swipe at the walls, knocking down spiders and webs and dirt. With each swipe he thought of all the bad things that had happened to him because of his sister. With each sneeze from the dust, he wiped his drippy nose with a sleeve and thought, *I hate you, Tabitha.*

After what seemed like hours, he turned to see his father looking at him. "I've just had a visit from the widow Shiphrah," Father said. "It seems you have knocked over her water pot and scattered her onions. Do you deny it?"

"No," he mumbled, his nose still dripping.

"Tomorrow you will go help her after synagogue. And you will not damage another's property again."

Without waiting for Seth to answer, his father walked away. Seth's anger, already burning like coals in his chest, flared hotter than ever.

———

At supper he was told to sit away from the family, alone. He could not hear the others' subdued conversation. He drank his water and ate his dinner of fresh-baked bread and fruit faster than usual. Tabitha's loud laughter didn't even make him jealous. He'd lost everything because of her; he certainly didn't want to *eat* with her.

After dinner he slept with his back to her. When he woke in the morning, he didn't even look at her as he left the room.

School was even worse than the day before. Joshua and David acted as if they didn't know him. The other boys laughed and teased him. *"Girl,"* he could hear them say. It was as if he had leprosy. No one wanted to be with him. They might catch the disease called "Tabitha."

That night before supper, Seth's mother sat him down underneath the olive tree. "You must speak to your sister and apologize."

Seth dug into the dirt with his toes. He ran his hand through his curly hair. He didn't want to apologize. He wasn't sorry; he wanted to do *more* to her!

Still, he nodded. He stood and went to his sister, who was weaving at the opposite end of the courtyard. He sat in front of her and glared at her. She gave him one of her smiles—the kind that reminded him she was glad for what she had done.

"What did you and your friends do for fun today?" Tabitha asked.

"I don't have any friends," Seth hissed.

She wove the yarn deftly in and out of the stretched threads. "*I* have *lots* of friends."

Seth bit his tongue. Then he took a deep breath and spoke. "I'm sorry I hit you!" he said loudly so his mother would hear.

Tabitha looked at him. Both of them knew he wasn't sorry at all—and neither was she.

———

The next day at synagogue school was no better.

He volunteered to stay after and sweep, just to give himself something to do.

When he got home, his mother looked worried. "Tabitha isn't well," she said. "I need your help. Could you please fetch the evening water from the well?"

Seth stared at her. *Girls'* work? "That's Tabitha's job," he said flatly.

"I told you, she's sick."

"Sure," Seth said sarcastically. *This is part of her plan to ruin my life*, he thought. *She can't wait to have the boys see me hauling water.*

His mother put her hands on her hips and tilted her head. "Whether you believe she is sick or not does not matter. She is not well enough to fetch the water. I cannot leave my supper. So you must go get it."

Seth picked up the large water pot from the kitchen area. He marched out the gate and through the town. He didn't look at anyone. He knew everyone had to be pointing and laughing. A grown boy fetching water? That was ridiculous!

He stood in line at the well, waiting his turn to get water. He was the only male in the group.

"How is your mother?" a woman named Rebekah asked.

"She is well," Seth muttered.

"And Tabitha?" the woman persisted.

"She claims to be ill," Seth said.

Rebekah raised one eyebrow, but said nothing more.

Seth filled his pot with water and tried to heft it onto his shoulder. It was heavy and awkward. He realized he'd never done anything with a water pot except tip it to pour water out. Struggling, he still couldn't lift it high enough.

"Let me help," Rebekah said kindly.

Seth let her, but his face burned with embarrassment.

He walked home slowly, trying not to drop the pot nor let too much water slosh out of it. By the time he reached home, his hair was completely wet and his tunic quite damp.

"Take this soup to Tabitha," his mother told him as he set the water pot down. She handed him a small bowl of warm broth.

Seth walked toward their room, but changed course when his mother wasn't looking. Behind the house he dumped the contents of the bowl into the dirt.

He went into the room. Tabitha lay there, asleep. He waited a few minutes, then returned the empty bowl to his mother. *If Tabitha wants supper, she can come out and eat with the rest of us and not be so lazy.*

———————

Three days passed. Seth fumed at his new tasks that only girls did. He fumed at Tabitha and her supposed illness. *She looks fine to me*, he thought. So she had a cough; so what? Didn't everyone have a cough at least once each winter? Why not in summer, too? She coughed at night and kept him awake, so he slept in the courtyard.

On the two occasions when his mother asked him to take broth to his sister, he dumped it on the ground behind the house. He overheard his parents speaking in worried tones about her. He was sick of seeing Eli every day with his eyebrows pulled together, asking how Tabitha was doing. "Don't worry," he wanted to say. "She's faking it to get attention."

On the Sabbath, after Seth and Father had returned from services, Tabitha called him into the room.

"Seth," she said, her voice weak.

Good job, Tabitha, he thought. *You're a great actress. Maybe you should move to Sepphoris and be in their plays.*

"I'm so sorry," she continued. " I was so mean to you and your friends."

Seth looked at her, believing her apology to be fake. At the very least Mother had probably made her do it.

"Really," Tabitha said, then paused as a coughing fit took over. Finally she spoke again. "I thought I was being funny."

"You have ruined my life," Seth told her flatly.

"I really am sorry," she said. Her voice was so quiet, Seth had to strain to hear her. "Until I got sick and couldn't see anyone but family, I didn't realize how important friends are. I thought you were making too much of your friends. But I was wrong, Seth."

He stared at her, not sure what to think. She was apologizing, but she certainly wasn't fixing anything.

"Will you forgive me?" she asked, her eyes pleading with him.

He looked right into those eyes, but said nothing. His anger kept guard around his heart, not letting anything in that might make him forgive her.

Without a word, he stood up and left.

S he is dying," the man said as he came out of the dark room.

Seth's mother clapped a hand over her mouth.

"You'd better send for her father."

Seth stared. This man was part of Tabitha's game, right? Sure, he was the doctor, but he had to be playing along. Tabitha only wanted sympathy. She wanted to get out of doing chores. She wanted Seth to continue to be the laughingstock of all the other kids.

Any minute, he thought, the doctor would laugh and tell them it was all a joke.

Seth waited. Nothing happened.

"Seth," his mother said, her voice choked with fear. "You heard the man. Go get your father."

Seth wanted to say, "But wait, it's only a joke." He ran into the room and knelt down to look closely at Tabitha. Her face was white and shiny with sweat. He touched her forehead, and it felt hot—like clay baking in the sun. Each breath sounded ragged and slow, like a heavy stone dragging through the dirt.

His throat tightened as he realized it was no joke.

He heard his mother's frantic voice behind him. "GO!" she shouted.

He turned and ran.

He ran blindly, not seeing anything except as obstacles. He dodged the obstacles—sometimes people, sometimes animals, sometimes a pot, sometimes a building. "Seth!" an old woman called. "Slow down! You'll hurt someone!"

I have already hurt someone, he thought. *I have hurt my sister.*

He ran on, taking the shortcut to the synagogue. But people clogged the streets, slowing him down. *Why are they here?* he thought. *What's going on?* He pushed through the people, ignoring their shouts.

I hurt someone. If she dies, it's my fault. He thought of the three times he had poured her broth into the dirt. Did the broth have some sort of healing medicine? Had he kept her from the medicine she needed?

He stopped. *Was it the lizard stew?* He felt sick. He started moving ahead. He ducked low and tried to move through the gathering crowd. The people seemed to draw closer and closer together. *I wished her dead. I wished my own sister dead.*

Guilt strangled him as he began to shove his fist into people's sides. Their surprise gave him the inches he needed to move ahead. Finally he burst through the last clutch of people and out the other side.

He ran up the last hill to the synagogue. "Father!" he called. "Father, come quick!"

His father appeared at the door of the synagogue. "What is it now, Seth? Are you in trouble again?"

Seth shook his head. "Tabitha's dying," he said, his voice squeaking.

His father looked down at the ground. "I must find him," his father said.

"Who?" Seth asked.

"Jesus. I must find Jesus." His father's face was etched with a worry and a desperation Seth had never seen.

He's not making sense, Seth thought, shaking his head. "Father, we must get home right away! Didn't you hear me? Tabitha is dying!"

"First we find Jesus. He can help us." His father's face twisted in grief. Tears formed in his eyes, then began to roll down his cheeks. Seth had never seen his father cry. Never.

And it's all my fault, Seth thought, feeling sick to his stomach.

He stared at his father's back as the man moved briskly down the hill. "Father!" Seth shouted, running after him. "Father, you must go home! What can a rabbi teach you now?"

When he reached his father, he held onto the man's sleeve. "Come on, Father. You must come this way."

His father shook him off.

Tabitha is almost dead, Seth wanted to shout. But the words would not come out. *I saw her. I know what dead looks like.*

He remembered the bird. He remembered the lizard. Dead things. Limp, with something missing. Tabitha was almost there. Why hadn't he realized it before? Why had he thought she was playing?

His father strode toward the crowd Seth had

moved through earlier. He, too, tried to break through. But many had gathered to follow Rabbi Jesus and hear what he had to say.

"Teacher!" someone called out. "Do we tithe a tenth of everything, including the broth we make, or only of our first fruits and animals?"

Seth did not hear whether or not the rabbi answered. He clung to his father's tunic, the handful of fabric absorbing the sweat of panic that had formed on his palms. He tucked his head down and let his father guide him.

"Rabbi!" he heard his father call.

There was no answer. So many calls of "Rabbi!" and "Teacher!" filled the air. Jesus would not hear their cry above the others. And what about his disciples? They were known to be rough men. Would they let them get anywhere near the rabbi?

"Rabbi!" his father called again.

Seth felt crushed by the people, all pushing to see Jesus. The earthy smell of warmth and bodies and garlic and olive oil was suffocating.

"Rabbi," his father said, falling at the feet of Jesus.

Seth, still standing, stared at his father. He had never seen his father so humbled before anyone. His father was an important man. He would never bow before anyone but . . .

Seth's eyes grew wider. *Anyone but God.*

His father cried out, his words tumbling fast. "My little daughter is dying. Please come and put your hands on her so that she will be healed and live."

Seth looked up into the rabbi's face. From what people had said about Rabbi Jesus, Seth had expected him to be extra tall, handsome, and powerful-looking. Yet this man looked like any other man from Galilee. Except for his eyes. There was something in his eyes. Seth wished he could say what it was. There was a strength, a kindness, a peace.

Without hesitation, Jesus agreed to come with them.

Seth hung back. He didn't want Jesus to see him. *What if this rabbi can tell what I've done?* he thought.

Seth couldn't hear any more of his father's words to the rabbi, nor the rabbi's words in return. People pressed in around them, calling to Jesus, wanting his attention.

Who is my father that this rabbi would pay attention to him while he doesn't seem to hear the voices of others? Seth wondered.

Suddenly the rabbi stopped. "Who touched my clothes?" he asked.

Seth looked around him. He could barely move with the crush of people. What did Jesus mean? Weren't lots of people touching his clothes?

One of the men who must have been Jesus' followers said, "You see the people crowding around you."

Rabbi Jesus acted as though he hadn't heard. He kept looking around him to see who had touched him. Then everyone else in the crowd took up looking.

Seth wanted to shout at the rabbi, "My sister is dying! And you wonder who touched you?" He wanted to whisper to his father that this rabbi was going to be of no help at all if he was going to stop every time someone bumped him. "Father!" he wanted to shout. "We need to go, *now!*"

A woman nearby fell at Jesus' feet. "I touched you," she said quietly. "I wanted to be healed."

The unclean woman, Mariah? He shook his head, disgusted. *She should know better.* Because she was unclean, she'd lived outside Capernaum since the day Tabitha was born. Seth's mother often took food to leave outside her home. Doctors traveling through were asked to examine her and see if they could help. But no one could.

Seth frowned. Since she had touched the rabbi's clothes, would he have to be unclean, too? He put his head in his hands. The rabbi was never going to get to Tabitha.

Seth lifted his head, just in time to see Jesus look straight into the woman's eyes. "Daughter, your faith has healed you."

Seth raised his eyebrows. She was healed? Just like that? Without medicine? Without a doctor?

"Go in peace and be freed from your suffering," Jesus said to her.

Hope jumped in Seth's chest. Jesus had healed Mariah? Everyone had talked about Mariah for as long as he could remember. The way she stood up straight and walked through the crowd, Seth knew she had to be healed. Maybe Jesus *could* heal Tabitha!

"Coming through!" Seth heard someone say. "Coming through. We must get to Jairus. We must get to the synagogue ruler."

The crowd parted until Seth's neighbors stood before his father. "Jairus," they said, "we bring you bad news. Your daughter Tabitha is dead."

CHAPTER 9

Seth's hope crashed. His stomach seemed to turn over, and it felt like someone had just slugged him in the head. Everything seemed wobbly, blurry.

His father's knees buckled, sending him to a kneeling position. But still the man looked up at Jesus as if asking for help.

Father, Seth thought, *dead is dead. Maybe Rabbi Jesus can heal people who are alive, but no one can reverse death. No one.*

One of the neighbors put his hand on the arm of Seth's father. "Why bother the teacher anymore?"

In the same way that Jesus had looked into the eyes of the woman, he looked into the eyes of Seth's father. "Don't be afraid, just believe."

Seth numbly watched his father nod at Jesus, his face full of hope and trust. Seth wanted so badly to trust as his father did. But he couldn't. *How can I trust this Jesus? He's only a rabbi. He's only a man.*

Seth looked up at the deep blue of the sky, as if he might find an answer. The sun was so strong it seemed to bake the top of his head. He touched his hair, and it felt hot. In this heat, bodies would begin to smell very quickly. The thought made him sick.

How could I have wished this on my own sister?

He stood there, letting the crowd flow around him, as people began to follow Jesus and his father toward his home.

Home? What would home be like without Tabitha? His mother would cry a lot, Seth guessed. Otherwise, it would be so quiet. He would have a room all to himself. None of the kids he knew had that.

Tabitha, he thought, almost as if he could talk to her. *I don't want my own room. Not like this.*

He walked toward home, his steps slow. Soon he noticed that the crowd was breaking up, the people shuffling off in several directions. Seth ran up to a small man and tugged on his tunic. "Excuse me," he said, "where is everyone going?"

"The teacher said no one could go with him. He will only let the father and three of his men go." The man shook his head and grumbled. "I don't know why he won't allow anyone else to come."

Seth felt more alone than ever. *I can't even go to my own house*, he thought.

He stood in the middle of the street, not knowing what to do.

"Hey, Seth," a voice behind him said.

Seth turned to see David standing there. David looked down his nose at him. "Do you think it was your sister's sin or the sin of your family that caused your sister to die?"

Seth glared at him. "It was *our* sin, David. *Our* sin."

David tipped his chin into the air and stomped off.

A hand rested on Seth's shoulder. "Do you think sometimes death just happens?" Joshua said into his ear. "Maybe it wasn't anybody's fault. A fisherman sees death all the time. And it just seems to be a part of living."

Seth knew Joshua was trying to be kind, but he couldn't stand to hear any more. Breaking through the crowd, Seth ran as fast as he could. He ran through the streets. He could hear the sounds of the mourners, already beginning their loud cries and wailing.

Not knowing where else to go, he ran toward the synagogue. He ran until his side ached and forced him to slow to a walk.

He stood under the portico, panting. Something inside him had changed. He could feel it.

It was as if a wall had fallen from around his heart. A wall of anger had protected his heart from feeling anything about losing Tabitha. But now the wall was gone, as completely as the wall had fallen from around Jericho. But when his wall fell, there seemed to be nothing inside.

It's like I died, too. I died inside. It felt strange that his body kept moving. It felt hollow. His eyes saw things, but it was like they didn't really see.

I hated Tabitha enough that she died. And I died, too.

He wandered away from the synagogue. Then, walking along the path, he left the village. He walked up the hill, not turning around to look at the lake or to walk backwards.

Hadn't he dreamed of this day for a long time? Hadn't he dreamed of his sister being gone forever, relished what it would be like without her telling him what to do?

But his mother was right. She'd said his sister

would be missed, and he missed her already. He would never see her again. He climbed a rock, sitting upon it, hugging his knees to his chin.

He could hear the wailing of the people below, the ones surrounding his house. The eerie sound crawled up the hill and under his skin. The women wailed, their moans and calls clouding the air, hanging thickly, covering all other sounds. They gave him chills, prickly sensations.

He put his hands over his ears and tried to keep out the sound. "It's my fault!" he screamed.

No one heard him, he knew.

He looked down at the village. He knew he should be there, but he couldn't go. He couldn't face his mother and father, knowing he was responsible for Tabitha's death. Hadn't his anger killed her? Hadn't his wish made her die?

He wondered why he couldn't cry. It was as if all the tears had turned to stone inside. They were there; he could feel them. But they wouldn't come out.

He dropped from the rock. He threw himself on the ground, his nose almost to the dirt. A memory came—of when he and Tabitha were very little. She had helped him when he'd fallen. She'd gently washed his bloody knee and elbow. She'd sung him a sweet little song, then sent him on his way.

A tear fell, making a dark spot in the dirt.

He remembered how so many times they had talked and laughed and giggled and told stories until his parents had to come to the door of their room and remind them to be quiet and go to sleep.

Another tear fell, and another.

"A new boy is in our village, Seth," she had told him once when he was small. "He looks a lot like you. Come with me. I'll introduce you." She had taken his hand and taught him how to wind around the houses to find the right one. Then she had said, "Hi, David. Here's my brother, Seth. You two will be in synagogue school together."

The tears came faster. His nose began to drip.

He remembered how she'd left him alone with David so that the two could become friends. They would have met in synagogue school in a few days, but she'd been kind enough to introduce them sooner. They had a chance to become friends first, so their first day of synagogue school wouldn't be quite so scary.

He let the tears fall into the dirt, not stopping

them. *I've been so wrong. She loved me. She was a pest, but she loved me.*

He'd done something terrible. He wanted to be forgiven. But there was no way he could get forgiveness from God. He was only a boy, and a boy could not offer a sacrifice. What would happen to him now? He deserved whatever punishment God decided on.

God, please forgive me, his heart screamed. But he could not pray it out loud. He was afraid to. Without a sacrifice, what right did he have to ask God to forgive? Without the shedding of the blood of a perfect animal, there would be no forgiveness.

Seth had never felt so hopeless in his life.

He thought his heart would break open. Then he thought it had. "Rabbi Jesus," he whispered to the air, "can you really heal? Can you make my sister alive again? If you can, will you? Please?"

He blushed, realizing he'd been fingering his prayer tassel. Had he been *praying* to a *rabbi*? Fear raced through him. *Blasphemy*. He looked around, and then up to the sky. God could punish him as He'd punished others in the old days who had done horrible things.

But the ground didn't open up and swallow him.

No fire from heaven fell to burn him up.

Instead of fear, he felt peace.

That was when he noticed something strange. The mourners had stopped. Mourners were paid to show how upset the family was that a loved one had died. How could they stop?

He jumped up, as if by standing he could hear better. *Not a sound of a single mourner*. They couldn't stop. Didn't they know how sorry he was? They *must* cry—long and loud.

He ran down the hill, slipping, stumbling. He ran, his chest hurting from breathing so hard.

His feet pounded the streets as he ran to his house. He turned a corner, and then he saw the mourners.

They were *laughing!* He shook his head. How could they laugh?

Getting closer, he listened. Finally he realized they were mocking someone. They were mocking the rabbi! He swallowed. Rabbi Jesus hadn't healed his sister? Is that why they were mocking him?

"Excuse me," he said to one of the mourners. "Why have you stopped crying?"

The woman threw up her arms and laughed to the sky. "The rabbi told us to stop! He told us the little girl was not dead, but asleep! As if we don't know what dead looks like! We have all seen her, and she is *dead*. I guess the rabbi has not seen death before." She cackled again.

Seth didn't know what to think. He wanted to hope Tabitha really *had* been asleep, that maybe he'd get another chance to be a brother to her—the kind of brother he knew he should have been. But mourners knew what death looked like, didn't they?

He ducked in and through the crowd of mourners. He felt the rough edges of cloth rub his face—and smooth linen when he passed those who were more wealthy. Most of them mumbled quietly, complaining about the rabbi.

When Seth reached the courtyard gate, a large man stopped him. "You can't go in there. Jesus has told everyone to stay outside."

"But that's my sister in there," Seth argued.

"And I'm his disciple, and I'm not even allowed in. Sometimes the Teacher prefers to do his work without people watching. He's not a show."

"Can he do it?"

The man smiled. "He is a man of surprises and power. We can only wait and see."

Moments later, the door opened. Seth's father

came out first, looking dazed. His mother was next. She ran to Seth and whispered, "Go find something to eat. Hurry. Soup, broth, anything. Perhaps Rebekah has something. She often begins cooking early."

"What happened?" Seth asked, his heart pounding.

"Just go. You will see when you return. Hurry!" Her eyes sparkled, and she seemed to be trying to hold back a smile.

CHAPTER 10

As he plowed through the crowd and into the street, Seth heard his father speaking. "You may all . . . go home. We do not need your services."

We do not need your services.

Could this be? Could it be that they didn't need the mourners *because there was nothing to mourn?*

Seth ran past three houses, then turned toward the lake and passed five more. "Rebekah," he called breathlessly as he reached the small house. "Rebekah. Do you have any soup? My mother needs some right away."

Without asking questions, the neighbor ladled some of her soup into a small, clay vase so it wouldn't spill. She handed it to him. Seth half walked, half ran back to his house.

In the courtyard, Jesus was speaking with his parents. There was Eli, too—standing apart, his face anxious, straining to hear what was being said. Mother looked at Seth and pointed toward his room.

He dashed inside. As his eyes adjusted to the darkness, he saw something that did not seem real. There sat Tabitha.

"I'm starved," she said. "Is that soup?"

Seth couldn't speak. He stared at her. He knelt by her pallet and handed her the soup. He watched as she took the vase and peered inside. "Any lizards?"

Seth shook his head.

"Any dirt? Or dead bugs?"

He shook his head again.

She put the vase to her lips and tipped it up. A few moments later she smacked her lips. "Mmm! Mother didn't make this, did she?"

Seth still couldn't find his voice. He shook his head. Was he dreaming this? Would he wake up in a minute to the sounds of the mourners wailing? Would he wake to find he really *did* have a room with no sister?

"It's good, but not as good as Mother's," Tabitha said, looking at him. "I am *so* hungry. I feel like I haven't eaten in . . . forever. How long have I been asleep?"

Seth shrugged his shoulders.

"What are you staring at?" Tabitha asked between sips.

Seth kept staring. His heart thumped. It jumped. It felt like maybe it was dancing. Now his insides were alive, but his outsides seemed dead.

"Do you want some? Is that why you're staring?"

Seth shook his head. A smile started slowly, then grew bigger. His voice finally woke up. "Are you feeling better?"

She lowered the vase and closed her eyes. A smile like he'd never seen took over her face. "I feel so perfect," she said, her voice soft. "A man was in here. He spoke to me, and it was like he reached into some sort of darkness and called to me. His hand sent a—a kind of power through me." She opened her eyes and looked at her brother. "Seth, I don't know what happened. I remember being so, so sick. I felt so awful, so weak, and so hot. And then I couldn't keep my eyes open any more. I couldn't breathe. I thought I stopped breathing. I thought everything just stopped."

"Then what?" Seth asked.

She shrugged. "I don't remember anything else."

She took Seth's hand. This time he didn't yank it away. He let her hold it. He *wanted* her to hold it.

"I feel good, Seth. I feel different. I'm all better."

"I'm glad," he whispered.

Now it was Tabitha's turn to stare. "What's wrong with you? I think you really *mean* that." She tilted her head. "Did mother make you say that?"

Seth gulped. "No." He looked down at the floor. "I do mean it," he said, his voice barely audible.

She drank a little more soup, watching him closely.

"I'm sorry," he said, his voice squeaking.

"What?"

"I'm sorry. I've been so mean to you."

Tabitha dabbed at her mouth with the back of her long tunic sleeve, still watching him.

"I shouldn't have made you sick with the lizard soup and embarrassed you," he said.

She nodded, listening intently.

"I still don't like that you always bother me and my friends. But . . ." He swallowed again. "Maybe it wouldn't have been so bad to let you listen." He said it, but he didn't know if he meant it.

"Seth," Tabitha said. "You are such a pesky little brother."

Seth couldn't believe it. His sister thought *he* was a pest?

"But I still like you anyway," Tabitha said, then tipped the vase to get the last of the soup. "Let's go outside. I think I hear Eli's voice."

"Now *there's* a pest," Seth mumbled, feeling like his whole self was returning to normal.

"What do you mean?" Tabitha asked, defensive.

Seth grinned. "He's been here every day asking about you. He's been very worried."

Tabitha stood. To Seth's surprise, she didn't even wobble.

"Do you need help?" Seth asked.

She shook her head. "No. It's so odd. I've never been so sick and gotten better so completely and so fast."

"Maybe it's not so odd," Seth said as they walked through the door. "Rabbi Jesus touched you."

Tabitha looked at him, questions in her eyes. "That was Jesus?" Her eyes scanned the courtyard. "Where is he?"

Seth looked around but didn't see him.

"Tabitha!" Eli said, approaching quickly. "Are you sure you are well? Should you be walking about?"

"Why does everyone treat me like I just came back from the dead?" Tabitha said.

Seth watched the adults exchange glances.

"You were . . . very sick," her mother answered.

Seth wondered why they didn't tell her. She *had* been dead. The wonder of it swept through him again. Then, without warning, he said, "I missed you while you were sick."

"No you didn't," Tabitha said.

"*I* did, too," Eli told her.

"Of course *you* did," Tabitha said, then shyly looked away at the ground.

"Where did Jesus go?" Seth asked.

His father looked out the courtyard gates, his voice far away. "I don't know."

"He told us to speak of this to no one," his mother added, looking directly at Seth.

"Why?" Seth asked, confused.

"He didn't say," his father answered. "But it is clear we must obey."

Seth nodded. He remembered what the disciple said: "He is not a show."

"Can we talk about it to each other?" Seth asked.

His parents looked at each other. "I think so," his father answered.

Eli tugged his robes around him. "If people knew what happened, there would be masses following him, tugging on him, wanting his attention. He would have no peace."

"Did he . . ." Seth began, looking at Tabitha.

The adults nodded.

"Did he what?" Tabitha demanded.

Mother moved to Tabitha's side and put her arm around her. "Sweetie . . . you were dead."

Tabitha's knees gave way, and Mother held her up. "No . . . but . . . no!" the girl's voice came out in a whisper.

"You *were* dead," Father said. "But Jesus touched you, called to you, and you came back to life."

"But how?" Tabitha asked.

Father knelt in front of her. "Jesus loved you. I could see it in his eyes. I could feel it in his voice." Tears began to trickle down his face, and he didn't even try to wipe them away. "I thought I could not go on if you were dead." He reached over and grabbed Seth's hand, and looked him in the eye. "If either of you was dead. I love you that much. But this Jesus—his love is even stronger somehow."

"I thought I was in the presence of God Himself," Mother said. She clapped her hand over her mouth and looked to the sky. Then she took her hand away. "Please, God. I mean no blasphemy. This Rabbi Jesus is from You. He must be."

Eli nodded, his voice barely audible. "Perhaps . . . Jesus is the Messiah."

At that moment, before anyone could speak, two faces peered around the wall. "Can we come in?" Joshua asked.

"Of course," Seth's father said, standing and quickly wiping the tears from his eyes. "Come on, David."

"We wanted to—" Joshua started. When he saw Tabitha, his mouth stayed open. His eyes grew wide; he stopped so fast, David ran into him.

David scowled at Joshua. "What's *your* prob—" When *he* saw Tabitha, *his* mouth also stayed open and *his* eyes grew wide.

"But you . . . you . . ." David said, pointing at Tabitha. He turned to Seth. "What kind of joke is this? You lied to us to make us feel bad, didn't you?" he accused.

Seth shook his head. "I didn't tell you anything," he reminded him. "Anything you know, you heard from somebody else."

David looked from Seth to Tabitha and back. He looked terribly confused.

Joshua's look of astonishment changed to realization. His grin grew wide. "Jesus," was all he said.

David's eyes narrowed. "Jesus keeps touching unclean things. My father won't be happy to hear about this." He turned and walked out the gate.

"This is . . ." Joshua started, then hesitated. "This is so *great!* My father is going to *love* this! Was Peter the fisherman here?"

Seth's father spoke. "I think so."

Tabitha wrinkled her nose. "I thought I smelled fish."

"I don't want to be rude," Joshua said. "But I really think I should go talk to my father. He thinks Jesus is someone special. Maybe even the Messiah. Would it be okay if I leave?"

"Go ahead," Seth's father said.

"I'm glad you aren't sick any more, Tabitha,"

Joshua called. "Really I am." Waving, he ran out the gate.

"I'm sure we'll have more visitors," Seth's mother said. "I'd better go prepare a feast."

"You may have one of my lambs," Eli offered. "I'll go prepare it now."

"I'll help," Seth's father said, and the two men strode away quickly.

Tabitha turned to Seth. "You know what?"

Seth shook his head. He still couldn't believe any of this was real.

"I'm glad you're my brother. And I'll miss you when I get married."

"You'll only be on the other side of town," Seth said. "We can still get together."

"I'll have you over for stew," she teased.

"I'll practice Torah with you."

Her eyes lit up. "Would you really? Eli has said he is not opposed to me learning all I wish. So you and I can learn together." She paused. "If you want."

"Maybe not all the time," Seth said. "I mean, I'm glad you're my sister, but I still don't want you bugging me every day."

"Do you think your friends would come back if I talked to them and promised to leave you alone?"

Tabitha asked. "I mean it. I won't bother you."

"I don't think one of them wants me for a friend. I think the other one might not care as long as you weren't *always* around."

Tabitha threw her arms around Seth, giving him a quick hug. "Oh," Seth said, "and not too much of that stuff, either."

Tabitha laughed. She reached over and ruffled his curls. "Let's go tell Mother we're not going to fight anymore."

"Well, not *most* of the time," Seth said, and smiled.

Letters From Our Readers

Is this story true? If so, where did you find it?

Curious George, Watertown, NY

The basis for this story is found in the New Testament of the Bible: Matthew 9:18–25, Mark 5:21–43, and Luke 8:40–56. If you read these, you will not find any story about Seth, only about Jairus (Seth's father) and his daughter (Seth's sister). We took the real Bible story and asked, "What if?" What if this girl was a pest and she had a younger brother who finally couldn't stand her anymore? We took what we knew about the real Bible story and what we knew about people and wrote a story so that you, the reader, could see that people in the Bible were just like us (only without all the extra "stuff" like computers, televisions, and telephones). The most important part of the story is the real part—about Jesus' love and power over death.

Why is there so much gross stuff in this story? A dead bird, maggots, lizard soup...

Signed, Misty A. Behr, Colorado Springs, CO

Sorry if we grossed you out! But a lot of kids are fascinated by things like that. We figured some kids in Bible times were the same way, and wanted the boys to seem real, not fake.

Okay, but did Tabitha HAVE to throw up?

M.A.B., Danbury, CT

Uh, well, I guess not...
Ed.

I'm confused. I thought a synagogue was like a church.

Trevor, San Rafael, CA

The synagogue was a place where the Jewish people held services on the Sabbath. Scriptures were read and men taught the people about them. During the week, they used the building for many other events—school, town meetings, whatever it was needed for. Jairus, the father of Tabitha and Seth in the story, was the synagogue ruler, or the *hazzan*. His job was to keep the synagogue in running order. People went to him for permission to use the synagogue. Sometimes the synagogue was even used for travelers who had no other place to stay.

People usually sat on the flagstone floor in the synagogue. Some sources say women sat separately from the men. Others say they sat together. One thing is for certain—the raised stone benches around the walls of the synagogue were for the important men of the village or the male visitors.

Were women really not supposed to learn?

Stacie Michaels, Milwaukee, Wisconsin

Israelite women were more respected than the women of some other Middle Eastern cultures. They were allowed to learn, and were supposed to learn the basics of Torah (God's Law) in order to teach their children. They needed to understand the holy days and festivals, for they had to know what to cook and why they were cooking the foods a particular way.

Since their responsibilities were many, they did not have time to go to school, nor were they invited to go to school. Their classroom was the home where they learned cooking, weaving, raising children, and so on.

Why did Tabitha and Seth share a room? Was their family poor? I wouldn't want to share a room with MY stinky, smelly, yucky sister.

Matthew Waisanen, Antioch, CA

Actually, their family was better off than most—so they had more rooms to their home. Most families had a home with one large room. A corner of it was the kitchen or cooking and storage area. Then they had another area where they rolled out their pallets and slept. Most kept the animals in the house with them at night. The animals had their own dirt area, which was lower than the living space for people.

As for sisters, they actually can be rather nice to be around. As Seth learned, family is important. God wants us to honor our family members, even when they get on our nerves.